Dear Parent:
Your child's love of reading

Every child learns to read in a different way and at his or her own speed. You can help your young reader improve and become more confident by encouraging his or her own interests and abilities. You can also guide your child's spiritual development by reading stories with biblical values and Bible stories, like I Can Read! books published by Zonderkidz. From books your child reads with you to the first books he or she reads alone, there are I Can Read! books for every stage of reading:

SHARED READING
Basic language, word repetition, and whimsical illustrations, ideal for sharing with your emergent reader.

BEGINNING READING
Short sentences, familiar words, and simple concepts for children eager to read on their own.

READING WITH HELP
Engaging stories, longer sentences, and language play for developing readers.

READING ALONE
Complex plots, challenging vocabulary, and high-interest topics for the independent reader.

ADVANCED READING
Short paragraphs, chapters, and exciting themes for the perfect bridge to chapter books.

I Can Read! books have introduced children to the joy of reading since 1957. Featuring award-winning authors and illustrators and a fabulous cast of beloved characters, I Can Read! books set the standard for beginning readers.

A lifetime of discovery begins with the magical words *"I Can Read!"*

Visit www.icanread.com for information on enriching your child's reading experience.
Visit www.zonderkidz.com for more Zonderkidz I Can Read! titles.

Choose for yourselves right now
whom you will serve.
—*Joshua 24:15*

www.zonderkidz.com

Super Ace and the Rotten Robots
Text copyright © 2009 by Cheryl Crouch
Illustrations copyright © 2009 by Matt Vander Pol

Requests for information should be addressed to:
Zonderkidz, *Grand Rapids, Michigan 49530*

Library of Congress Cataloging-in-Publication Data

Crouch, Cheryl, 1968-
    Super Ace and the rotten robots / story by Cheryl Crouch ; pictures by Matt Vander Pol.
        p. cm. -- (I can read! Level 2)
      ISBN 978-0-310-71697-6 (softcover)
      [1. Superheroes--Fiction. 2. Christian life--Fiction.] I. Vander Pol, Matt, 1972- ill. II. Title.
    PZ7.C8838Su 2009
    [E]--dc22
                                                  2008038644

Art Direction & Design: Jody Langley

Printed in China

10 11 12 /SCC/ 4 3

ZONDERkidz **I Can Read!**™

Super Ace and the Rotten Robots

story by Cheryl Crouch

pictures by Matt Vander Pol

Super Ace and Sidekick Ned
flew through deep, dark space.

BEEP! BEEP! BEEP!

"It's my super phone.

Planet Roop is calling!"

said Super Ace.

Rooper met them on Roop.

"Will you help us, Super Ace?"

He did not ask Ned.

Ned was just a sidekick.

Super Ace smiled.

"I can help. I am a superhero.

What is wrong on Planet Roop?"

A robot bopped Rooper on the head.
"Ouch! Our robots used to help us,
but now they are mean."

A robot broke Ned's music player.

"Hey! That was rude," Ned said.

Super Ace frowned.

"These rotten robots

should choose to be good."

Ned said, "Robots cannot choose."

"Sidekick Ned, you forget,

I do not need your help,"

said Super Ace.

Super Ace stood on a tall rock.

"Robots, see me use my superpower.

It is good looks."

He fixed his smooth, shiny hair.

He smiled a big, white super smile.

The robots looked at him.

"Choose to be good, not bad,"

said Super Ace.

The robots cheered for Super Ace.

He said, "See? I fixed the robots."

A robot threw a rotten tomato

right at Super Ace.

It landed in his smooth, shiny hair

with a SPLAT.

The robots laughed.

They threw more yucky things

at Super Ace.

"You are very bad robots!" he said.

"My good looks did not work,
so I will use my other power."
Super Ace picked up a robot.
"I am Super Ace," he yelled.
"I am super strong.
Do what I say, or I will throw you."
He threw a robot a long way.
The robot crashed to the ground.
BANG!
The other robots were afraid.

"You must do what I say,"

said Super Ace.

"Be good, okay?"

The robots cheered.

Super Ace turned to Rooper.

"See? The robots will be good now."

The thrown robot stood up.

He made an ugly face at Super Ace.

All the robots went crazy.

They hurt people and broke things.

"You have too many bad robots,"

Super Ace told Rooper.

"I can't make them be good,"

said Super Ace.

Rooper asked Ned, "Can you help?"

"Ha!" Super Ace laughed.

"Sidekick Ned is small and weak.

How can he control bad robots?"

"It is true that I am small,

but God makes me wise," said Ned.

"Can you make the robots choose

to be good?" Rooper asked.

Sidekick Ned shook his head.

Super Ace said, "See?

Sidekick Ned cannot help you."

Ned said, "I can help.
I cannot make robots choose,
but that is not the real problem.
See that big Robot Switch?"

GOOD

BAD

26

Ned walked to the control panel.

"This Robot Switch got moved

from Good to Bad.

I will fix it."

Sidekick Ned pushed the switch up.

The robots stopped throwing

and breaking and hurting.

They started to clean up the mess.

Ned said, "The robots are good now!"

Rooper looked at Sidekick Ned.

"Robots cannot choose, but we can.

I am glad you chose to help us!

Thank you," said Rooper.

"You are welcome!" said Super Ace

in a big, strong voice.

"And now that your robots are good,

I must help others who need me."

Rooper smiled and shook Ned's hand.

Then Super Ace and Sidekick Ned flew back into deep, dark space.